This book
belongs to

....

Tips for Reading and Sharing

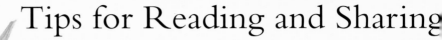

The Caterpillar That Roared is an engaging story about wanting to be different. Hugo the caterpillar longs to be a lion, but soon he finds out that being himself is not so bad after all.

Read on to find out how to get the most fun out of this story.

Snazzy word sounds

Enjoy the way the words sound! Look for passages where you can join in with Hugo as he practices growling like a lion. Make the most of exciting lines such as *"Ferdinand saw a HUGE and fearsome creature twitching its great whiskers, tossing its great mane, swishing its great tail."* Reading with a touch of drama can really help children get fully involved in the story.

Listen, look, and share

Let your child take charge and turn the pages. Encourage her to join in with repeated sentences such as *"I'd be frightened of you if you were a lion."* Point to the words as you read them together. Your child will want to do more as she gets to know the story.

Caterpillar dreams

Discussing the story is a good way to spend time together and will encourage your child to use her imagination. Talk about why Hugo would want to be a lion instead of a caterpillar. What are your child's special dreams? Discuss how Hugo feels when he frightens his friend Ferdinand. How does Hugo feel at the end of the story when he is with his friends again?

Picture clues – animal sizes

Look carefully at the scale of the animals in the pictures. Look at the size of Hugo and think about how big a lion would be. It wouldn't even fit on the page! No wonder the snail, the spider, and the tortoise think Hugo's dream is funny!

Enjoy the story –
and the dreams too!

Bernice E. Cullinan

Bernice E. Cullinan
Reading Consultant

For Cameron who is already a lion.
With much love, M.L.

For Viv, many thanks, A.B.

Dorling Kindersley Publishing, Inc.

95 Madison Avenue
New York, New York 10016

Library of Congress Cataloging-in-Publication Data
Lawrence, Michael (Michael C.)
The caterpillar that roared / by Michael Lawrence; [illustrated by Alison Bartlett]. – 1st American ed.
p. cm. – (Share-a-story)
Summary: Hugo the caterpillar tries to convince his friends that he is a lion until the day he
frightens Ferdinand the fish away and realizes that it is better to be himself.
ISBN 0-7894-6351-2 (hardcover)
ISBN 0-7894-5618-4 (paperback)
[1. Caterpillars–Fiction.   2. Animals–Fiction.   3. Self-Acceptance–Fiction.]
I. Bartlett, Alison, ill. II. Title.   III. Share-a-story (DK Publishing, Inc.)
PZ7.L4368 Cat2000 [E]–dc21 99-049689

Color reproduction by Dot Gradations, UK
Printed in Hong Kong by Wing King Tong

First American Edition, 2000

2 4 6 8 10 9 7 5 3 1

Published in Great Britain by Dorling Kindersley Limited.

Acknowledgments:
Series Reading Consultant: Wendy Cooling **Series Activities Advisor:** Lianna Hodson
Photographer: Steve Gorton **Models:** Vanity Garrikk, Joe Eytle, Cherise Stephenson, Sam and Danielle Bromley
U.S. Consultant: Bernice E. Cullinan, Professor of Reading, New York University

For our complete
catalog visit
www.dk.com

The Caterpillar That Roared

by Michael Lawrence

illustrated by

Alison Bartlett

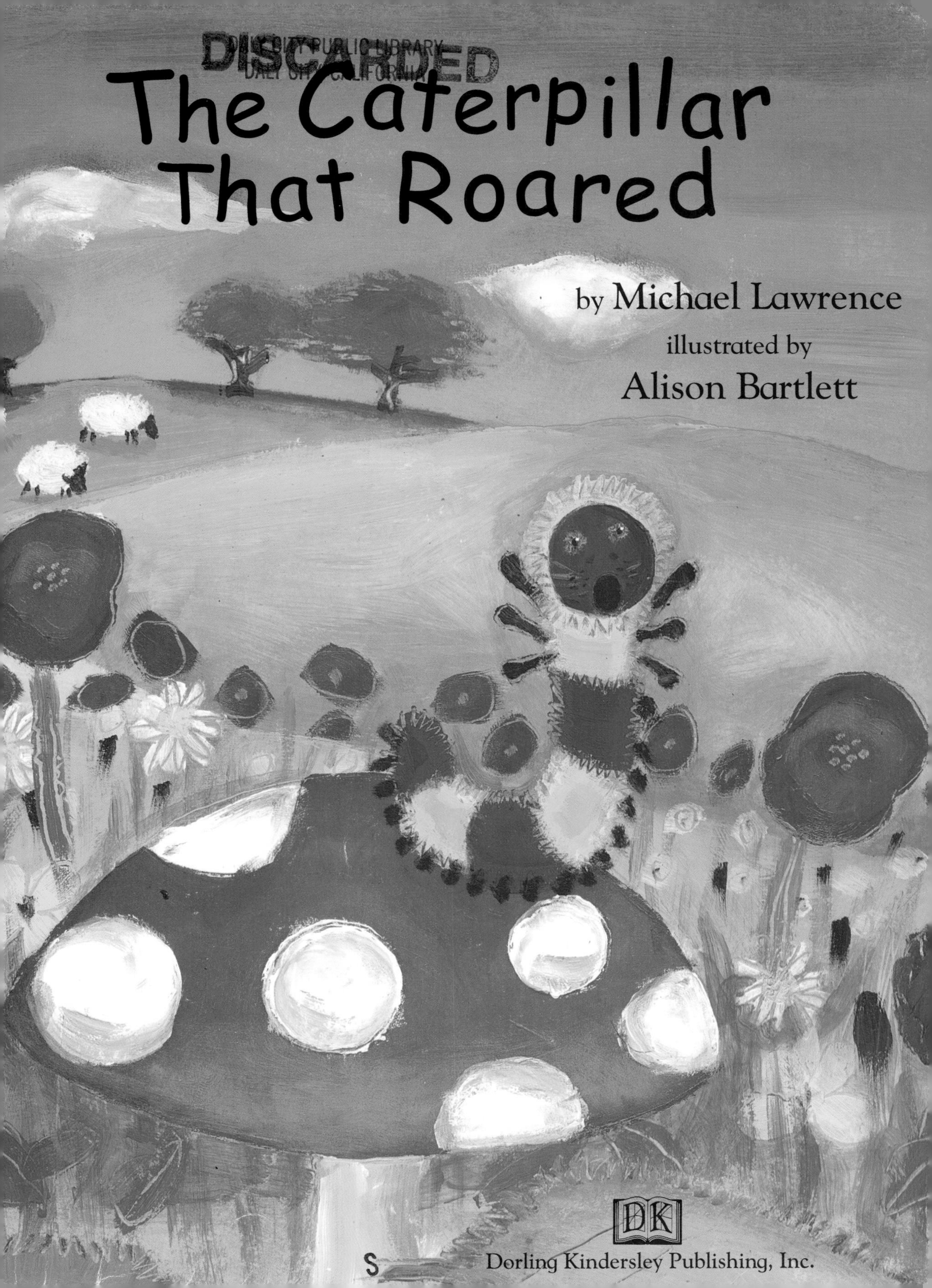

DK

Dorling Kindersley Publishing, Inc.

Some caterpillars want to be moths when they grow up, and some want to be butterflies. But Hugo wanted to be a lion.

Every morning when he woke up he would gaze at himself in the mirror to see if he looked like a lion.

He would pull himself up as tall as he could,

toss his imaginary mane...

...twitch his imaginary

whiskers

...and swish his imaginary tail.

But it was no good.
He still looked exactly
like a caterpillar.

So he practiced his **roar**.
At first the growl sounded
more like a squeak.

But he practiced and practiced,
and soon it began to sound like a
very small, very squeaky
little growl.

growl

Hugo decided to show off
his growl to his neighbors.

Winona the snail sat nearby.
Hugo growled at her.
"What a funny noise for a caterpillar to make,"
Winona said.

"I'm not a caterpillar," Hugo told her.
"I'm a lion."
Winona smiled. "No, no," she said. "Not you.
I'd be frightened of you if you were a lion."

Next he met Ollie the Spider, lying in the sun. Hugo growled. Ollie frowned. "Are you feeling all right, Hugo? I've never heard a caterpillar make a noise like that." "I'm not a caterpillar," Hugo said, "I'm a lion."

Ollie shook with laughter.
"That's the funniest thing I've heard all day.
You're no lion, sonny. I'd be frightened of
you if you were a lion."

Hugo went on his way, practicing his tiny growl, and met Ruby the Tortoise returning from shopping. It had taken her three days to get there and back and she was very tired.

Hugo *growled* at her.

"I'm a lion,"

he said
proudly.

"Oh, are you, now?" Ruby said.
"Well, all I can say is it's just as well you're not.
I'd be frightened of you if you were a lion."

Hugo gazed up at the grass and flowers growing high above him. "If I were a lion," he said, "I'd be **taller** and **bigger** than the whole wide world."

He tried to stretch himself up and puff himself out but it didn't work.

Even when he shut his eyes he didn't feel any bigger.

He sat down on the riverbank and looked at himself in the clear water. He hoped to see a great big lion there, but all he saw was a little caterpillar.

"*It's not fair!*" he wailed.
"Lions can be lions, so why can't *I* be one?"

Below the surface, Ferdinand the fish
was preparing his dinner. Suddenly he
saw something moving up above.

Through the ripples Ferdinand saw . . .

a huge and fearsome creature
 twitching its great whiskers,
  tossing its great mane,
   and swishing its great tail.

And then he heard . . .

...growl.

A great and terrible growl.

"*It's a lion!*" cried Ferdinand in fright, and he swam away as fast as he could.

Hugo was horrified.

"Come back, Ferdinand!" he shouted.
"It's me, Hugo. I'm not really a lion!"
But it was too late. Ferdinand was gone.

Hugo went home thinking about what had happened at the river. "If I was a lion," he said to himself, "everyone would run away from me. They wouldn't even stop to say hello."

And that night, as he snuggled down
to sleep, he thought, "I'm *glad*
I'm a caterpillar."

Activities to Enjoy

I f you've enjoyed this story, you might like to try some of these simple, fun activities with your child.

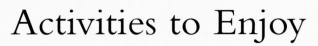

Ooooo Oooo

Flutter Flutter

Roar!

Animal make-believe

Ask your child what animal she would like to be and why. Imagine you're one, too. Then both pretend to be those animals. Flutter your wings like a butterfly, roar like a lion, or make a noise like a monkey. What does your animal eat? Where does it live? If you like, keep the game going by pretending to be a different animal.

Caterpillar puppet

Cut out several circles from colored paper. Overlap the circles slightly and tape them together, or use paper fasteners so the caterpill can move. Tape straws, wooden skewers, or Popsicle sticks on either end to use as handles. Finally, paint or draw a face on one of the end

Butterfly pictures

What will Hugo look like when he turns into a butterfly? Cut out a simple shape of a butterfly from a large sheet of paper. Fold the butterfly in half to make a crease and ask your child to paint one side of the butterfly. When she is finished painting, your child can fold the paper along the crease so the paint transfers to the other half. Then open the paper to see a beautiful butterfly!

Nature hunt

Why not look for caterpillars and butterflies in your garden or in the park? Or take a trip to the library to find out more.

Other Share-a-Story titles to collect:

Neil's Numberless World by Lucy Coats,
illustrated by Neal Layton

Not Now, Mrs. Wolf! by Shen Roddie,
illustrated by Selina Young

Are You Spring? by Caroline Pitcher,
illustrated by Cliff Wright

9/24 6/03   10-18-03